Say Something

Say Something

by Mary Stolz

illustrated by Alexander Koshkin

HarperCollinsPublishers

Say Something

Text copyright © 1968, 1993 by Mary Stolz

Illustrations copyright © 1993 by Aleksandr Koshkin

Printed in the U.S.A. All rights reserved.

Typography by Daniel C. O'Leary

1 2 3 4 5 6 7 8 9 10 ❖

Revised and Newly Illustrated Edition

Library of Congress Cataloging-in-Publication Data

Stolz, Mary, date

   Say something / by Mary Stolz ; illustrated by Alexander Koshkin.—Rev. and
newly illustrated ed.

     p.   cm.

   Summary: While out on a fishing trip with his son, a father is asked to "say
something" about the moon, night, sky, wind, caves, brooks, and many other
things that surround us in nature.

   ISBN 0-06-021158-X. — ISBN 0-06-021159-8 (lib. bdg.)

   I. Koshkin, Alexander, ill.   II. Title.

PZ7.S875854Say 1993   92-8317

[E]—dc20   CIP

                                                                        AC

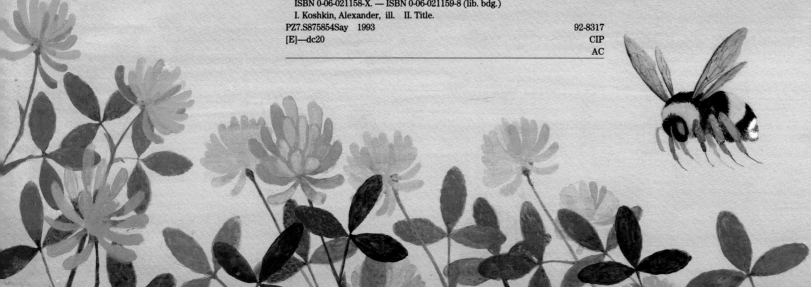

To Peg, and to her children:
Michael, Tom, Tris, Brian, John

M.S.

I dedicate my illustrations in this book
to my father, with whom I wandered so many
times with fishing tackle along lake and riverbank.

A.K.

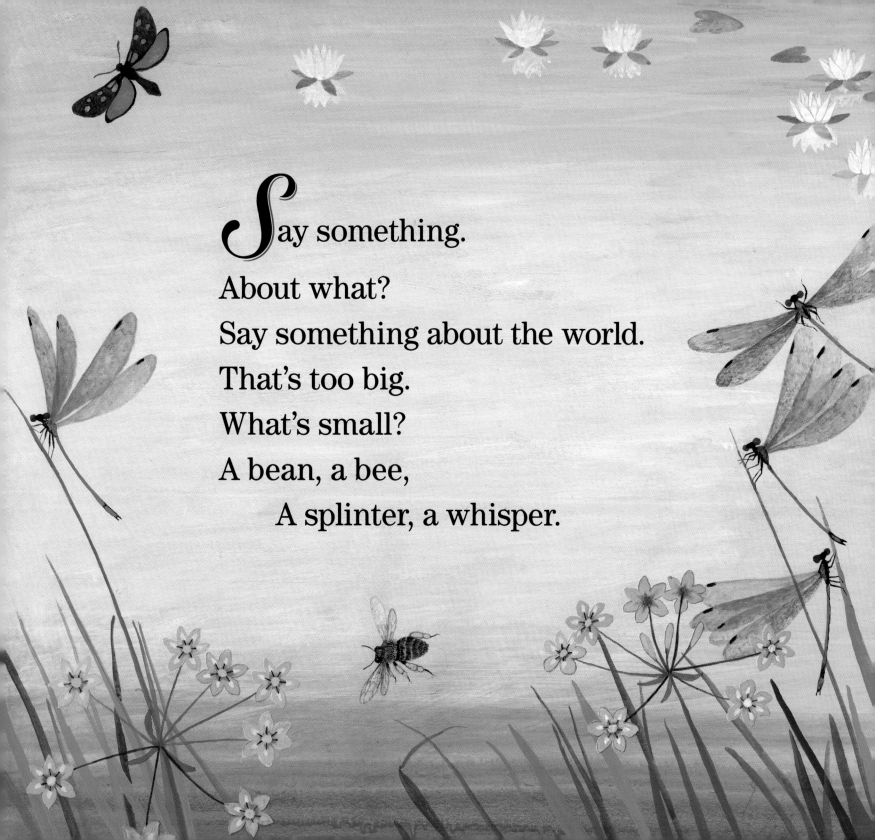

Say something.

About what?

Say something about the world.

That's too big.

What's small?

A bean, a bee,

A splinter, a whisper.

Say something about a cave.

A cave is a dark deepness.
It is a place to get lost in
and a place to find your way out of.

Say something about the grass.

The grass is a green living room
Where the toad, the cricket, the snake,
and the mouse live out their grass-high days.

Say something about a brook.

A brook is a watery hallway
Where the fish and the otter
Swim up and down peering in doorways.
What are the doorways?
Holes in the bank where kingfishers live.

Say something about a tadpole.

A tadpole is a brown bead on a string.
It's all right to call her a pollywog.

Say something about the sea.

All day the sandpiper plays tag with the sea.
"You're it, ocean!"
"I'm it—flee!"

Say something about a road.

A road meets another road that meets
Another road that meets another road.
There is no end to a road.

Say something about a mountain.

A mountain lasts forever.
It covers its slopes with trees and snow,
and inside it has a secret.
What's the secret?
A secret.

Say something about snow.

Snow is a shawl for the north wind's shoulders.

Say something about the wind.

It blows around the earth
and can come down the chimney.

Say something about the sky.

The sky is a hat.
Who wears it?
We all wear the sky.

Say something about the moon.

The moon is waiting for another footstep.

Say something about the night.

Night is a tunnel to morning.
It is lined with pictures.

Say something about me.

It's all about you.
And about me.
It's about all of us, everywhere,
Whirling in space.